First published in 2008 by Simply Read Books www.simplyreadbooks.com

Text © 2008 Anne Renaud    Illustrations © 2008 Geneviève Côté

LIBRARY AND ARCHIVES CANADA CATALOGUING IN PUBLICATION

Renaud, Anne, 1957-

Missuk's snow geese / Anne Renaud ; illustrator, Geneviève Côté.

ISBN 978-1-894965-82-8

I. Côté, Geneviève, 1964- II. Title.

PS8635.E518M58 2008          jC813'.6          C2007-905125-1

We gratefully acknowledge the support of the Canada Council for the Arts, the Government of Canada through the Book Publishing Industry Development Program, and the BC Arts Council for our publishing program.

Book design by Elisa Gutiérrez

10 9 8 7 6 5 4 3 2 1

Printed in Singapore

To my family with whom I lived the North.—AR

For Adrien—GC

Geneviève Côté wishes to thank le Conseil des arts et des lettres du Québec for its financial support.

# Missuk's Snow Geese

Anne Renaud

·

illustrations by

Geneviève Côté

·

·

·

·

·

simply read books

This story happened many springs ago in the land under the Northern Lights, home to the snow goose, the polar bear and the caribou.

"When will I be a great carver like you?" asked Missuk as she watched her father harness the five huskies to their dogsled.

"In time," her father answered. "It takes much practice, and you are still very young. When I return from the hunt, we will carve together."

Missuk helped load the dogsled with hunting spears, seal meat for the dogs to feed on, and dried fish for her father to eat. Then she waved her father off as he glided away on the snow.

When the dogsled was nothing more than a black speck on the horizon, Missuk crawled back into her igloo.

Sitting at her mother's side, Missuk watched as she cut a large mitten shape, a palm, and a thumb shape from a swatch of seal skin, then began to sew the pieces of fur together with a needle made of caribou bone. Missuk followed her mother's movements carefully and cut smaller shapes out of the seal skin. Then she too began sewing her pieces together.

But Missuk much preferred the cool smoothness of soapstone between her fingers rather than the hairs of seal fur.

So Missuk pulled one of her father's small goose carvings from her pocket and ran her fingers over its surface. Then she took a piece of raw soapstone and, with her ulu knife, tried to do as her father had taught her. But she could not find the graceful bird in the stone.

Frustrated, Missuk left her carving and her sewing behind and went outside.

The snow crunched under Missuk's seal skin boots as she walked across the frozen tundra. The darkness of the long winter months had finally retreated and the smell of spring was on the wind. Now, the sun hung above the horizon all day and almost all night.

Atop a small hill, Missuk lay in the snow and gazed up into the deep vastness of sky and at the spearheads of snow geese that streaked across its canvas. Moving her arms as though she too was taking flight, Missuk closed her eyes and imagined she was one of the beautiful geese her father carved from stone. When the geese flew low, Missuk tried to count them before they vanished from sight. And when their thunderous honks filled her ears, Missuk honked back, welcoming the migrating flocks home.

For many hours Missuk made a game of lying in
the snow and leaving her bird-shaped imprints
along the trail her father's dogsled had left
earlier that day.

When a fierce wind blew, Missuk knew a storm
was on its way and it was time to return home
to her mother.

Sheltered from the gales that twirled the snowflakes into blurry white spirals, Missuk listened for sounds of her father's dogsled. But none came.

"Your father is a skilled hunter and will be home soon," said her mother when Missuk could no longer stay awake and slid under her caribou skins to sleep. But Missuk saw the worry in her mother's eyes, for she also knew the cold could be unforgiving.

When sleep came, Missuk dreamt her father was lost amidst the blinding sheets of snow.

Then she dreamt his dogsled had broken through the ice and he and their huskies were helplessly sinking into the dark waters of the river.

Missuk woke with a start. Her heart beat hard in her chest until she saw her father's bear-like shape lying under his caribou skins.

"Your father is very tired," whispered Missuk's mother. "Come and we will unload the dogsled together while he sleeps."

Missuk followed her mother outside where together they emptied the dogsled of its fur skins, hunting spears, and caribou meat her father had brought back from the hunt.

When Missuk's father finally opened his eyes, this is the story he told.

"I found a herd of caribou and was able to kill one before they stampeded off across the plain," he said.

"Suddenly, a fierce wind blew. I could see
nothing but white. I would have been lost
had I not come upon a trail of goose shapes
stamped into the snow. These birds led me
across the tundra and up to a hilltop from
where I saw our igloo. This is how I found
my way home."

And at that moment Missuk knew, in time, she would be a great carver, for she too could make snow geese, just like her father.

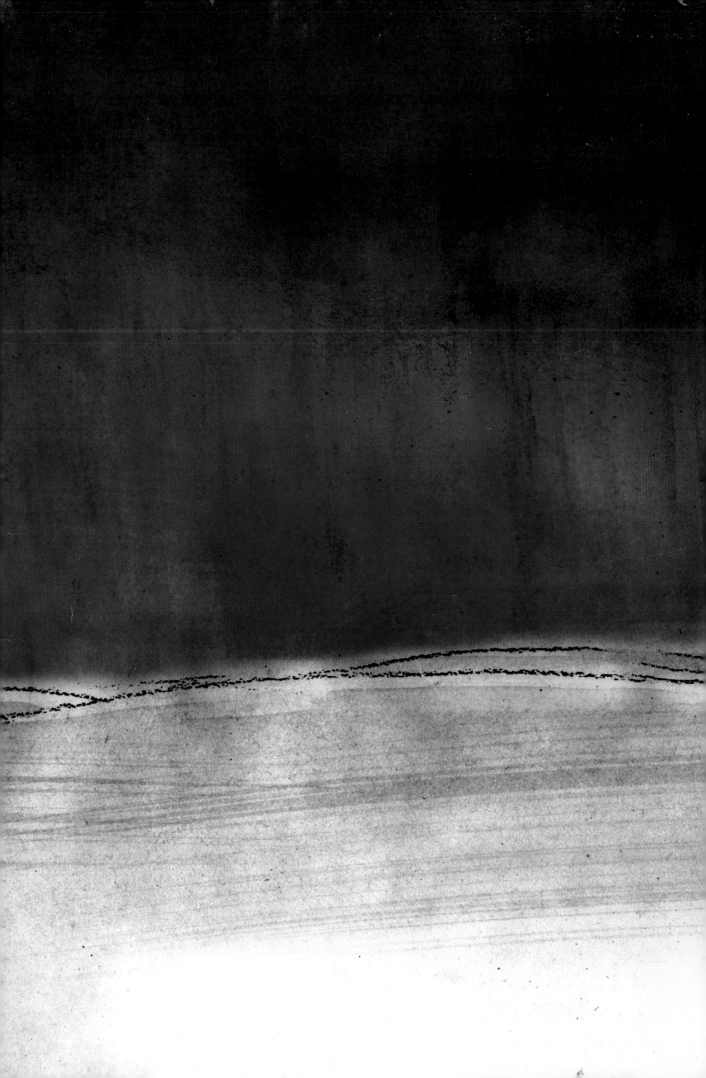